The Whole Night Through

a lullaby

Story and Woodcuts by
David Frampton

HARPERCOLLINS*PUBLISHERS*

The moon's sweet lullaby of light
falls softly through the jungle night
down past the leafy bongo tree

where everyone's asleep but me!

The rhino nestles in his bed
an egret perched upon his head

the crocodile is sleeping too

the kinkajou

the cockatoo

They're sound asleep across the land
If you're not sleepy raise your hand!

Goldfish, guppies and piranhas

monkeys dreaming of bananas

hogs in bogs

and pollywogs

I'm staying up the whole night through
I really think that you should too

The snake is sleeping peacefully
like ribbon candy in a tree

lazy lions side by side . . .
Are your peepers open wide?

zebras sleeping toe to toe

the wildebeest

the buffalo

the eland and the antelope

but am I sleeping? Nope!

In a leafy glade a mouse reposes

elephants' entwining noses

the hare

the hippopotamus

but not us!
We're staying up from dusk till dawn
wink . . . blink . . . . . . yawn

Beneath the leafy canopy
snooze butterfly

bumblebee

and me

And me!? Can it be so?
Sshushhhhhhh . . .
I am asleep you know

The moon still beams its milky light
where NO one's staying up tonight!
Now I know what we should do
Let's sleep and dream
the whole night through

good night

To my children, Sarah and David

The Whole Night Through: A Lullaby
Copyright © 2001 by David Frampton
Printed in the U.S.A. All rights reserved.
www.harperchildrens.com

Library of Congress Cataloging-in-Publication Data
Frampton, David.
The whole night through: a lullaby / by David Frampton.
    p.   cm.
    Summary: A leopard cub stays awake while the animals
in the jungle sleep the whole night through.
    ISBN 0-06-028825-6. — ISBN 0-06-028826-4 (lib. bdg.)
    [1. Leopard—Fiction.   2. Jungle animals—Fiction.
3. Sleep—Fiction.   4. Stories in rhyme.]   I. Title.
PZ8.3.F835Wh 2001   99-41338
[E]—dc21   CIP

          1 2 3 4 5 6 7 8 9 10
                        ❖
                  First Edition